C8   D0247659

To the memory of Seymour Regent and Sharon Clair
and for all my insomniac friends – M.B.

For John and Avis – N.M.

- M
30 A

- 1 JUN

First published in 2007
by Hodder Children's Books

First published in paperback in 2008

Text copyright © Mara Bergman 2007
Illustration copyright © Nick Maland 2007

Hodder Children's Books
338 Euston Road
London NW1 3BH

Hodder Children's Books Australia
Level 17/207 Kent Street
Sydney, NSW 2000

The right of Mara Bergman to be identified as the author and Nick Maland as the illustrator of this
Work has been asserted by them in accordance with the Copyright, Designs and Patents Act 1988.

All rights reserved

A catalogue record of this book is available from the British Library.

ISBN: 978 0 340 89329 6
10 9 8 7 6 5 4 3 2

Printed in China

Hodder Children's Books is a division of Hachette Children's Books
An Hachette Livre UK Company

Hodder
Children's
Books
A division of Hachette Children's Books

BIRMINGHAM LIBRARIES
SUTTON CHILDREN'S LIBRARY
C8/374
838
JJ
APRIL 08

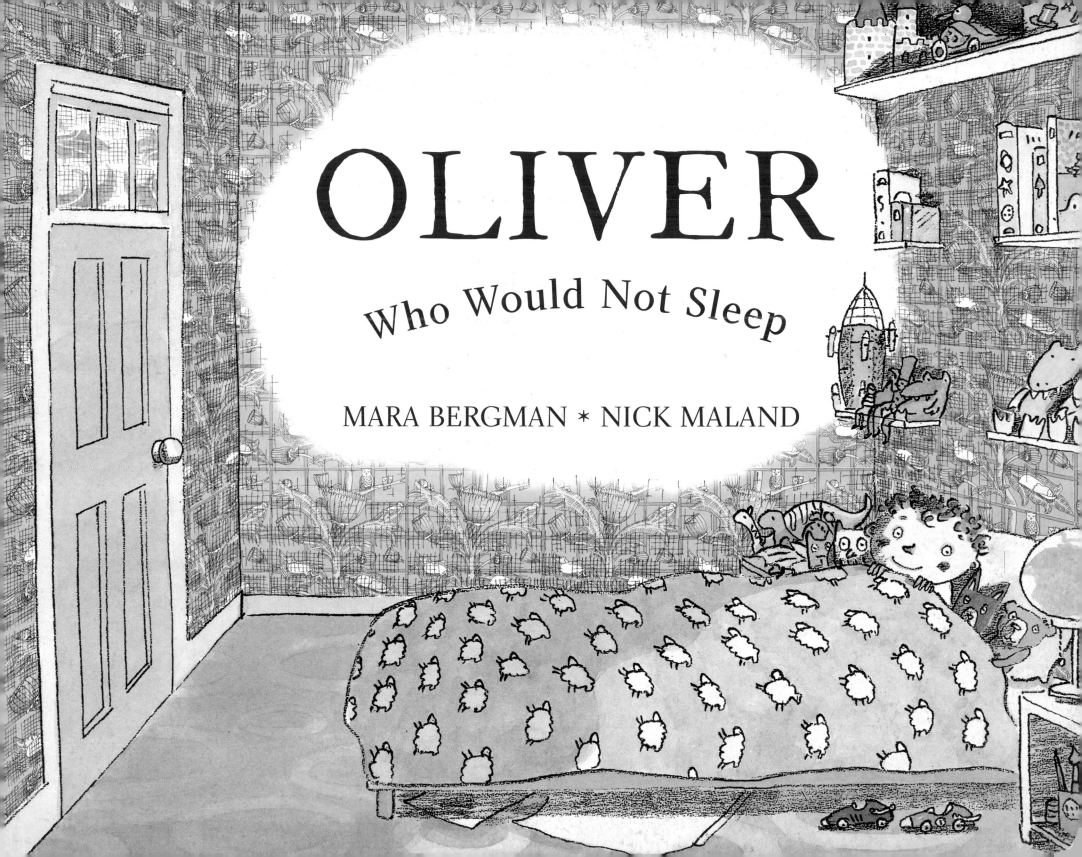

OLIVER

Who Would Not Sleep

MARA BERGMAN ∗ NICK MALAND

Oliver Donnington Rimington-Sneep

COULDN'T and DIDN'T

and WOULD NOT SLEEP!

It wasn't that he
was afraid of the dark,
of monsters or robbers
or sounds from the park,

but that...

Oliver Donnington Rimington-Sneep
liked staying awake
more than going to sleep.

After his parents had said goodnight,

they tucked him in and turned off the light.

Straight away Oliver bounced out of bed.

He painted...

and drew...

did magic...

and read.

He raced his cars,

then he raced them some more,

and just as he blasted his rocket he saw...

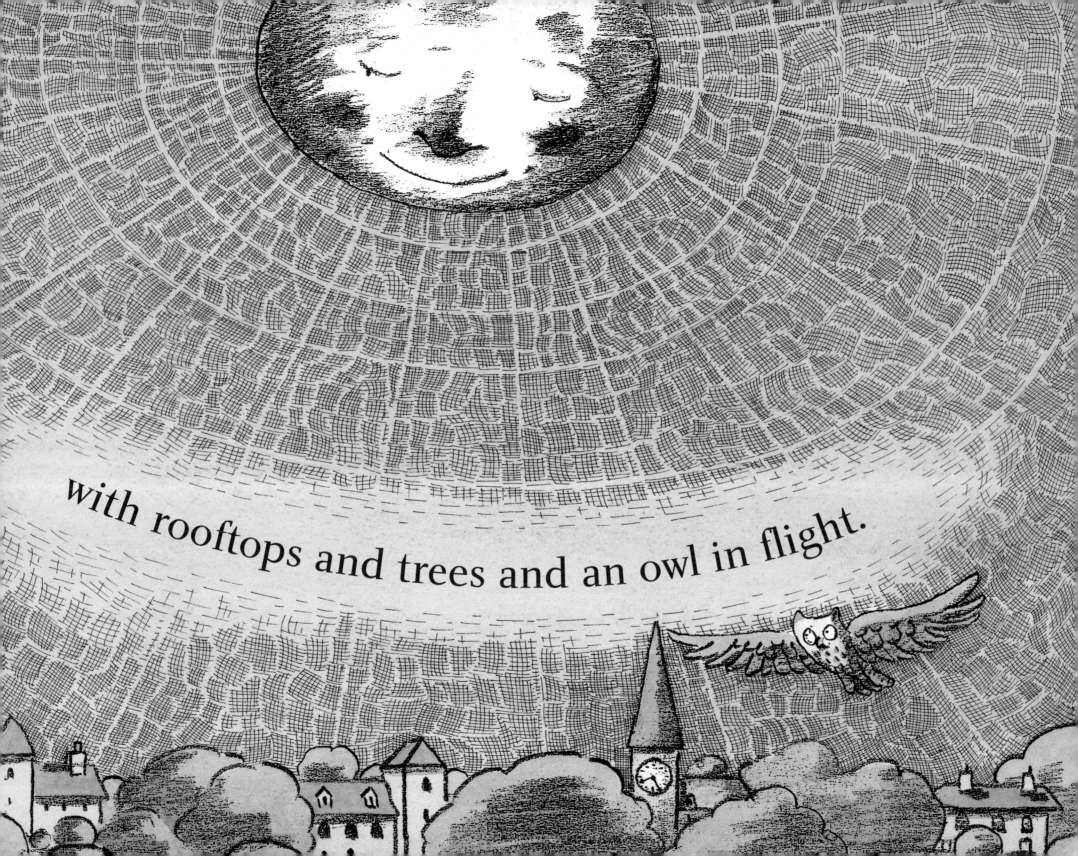

with rooftops and trees and an owl in flight.

Then Oliver's rocket flew fast and flew far, over houses and cities and up to the stars, past the moon and past comets till...

it landed on **Mars** –
a quiet and gigantic place
smack in the middle
of darkest space.

Oliver stood in amazement
and Oliver stared,
without even being
the slightest bit scared.

Suddenly, a streak of light
across the sky was shining bright.
Oliver saw his house far away
and wanted to go back home to play.

Through outer space,

over mountains and seas,

through clouds, over rooftops

and the branches of trees…

the rocket soared back to Oliver's room,
where all of his cuddlies looked cosy and warm.

Bat and Owl, Fox and Ted
were waiting for him to climb into bed.

So with a great big stretch

and a great long yawn...

Oliver Donnington Rimington-Sneep

finally... finally...

finally... finally...

fell fast asleep.